Princess Truly

I Am a Super Girl!

BY
Kelly
Greenawalt

ART BY
Amariah
Rauscher

ACORN™
SCHOLASTIC INC.

For my favorite super girls: Calista, Kaia, Ansley, Alison, Gabriella, and Audrey — KG

To Junie and Jalen. You are SUPER GIRLS. — AR

Text copyright © 2019 by Kelly Greenawalt
Illustrations copyright © 2019 by Amariah Rauscher

ISBN 978-1-338-84590-7

10 9 8 7 6 5 4 3 2 1   22 23 24 25 26

Printed in the U.S.A.   40

This edition first printing April 2022

Edited by Rachel Matson and Liza Baker
Book design by Sarah Dvojack

Truly Super

I am Princess Truly.
I am a super girl.

I put on my rocket boots

and give my cape a twirl.

I am very mighty.

I am strong and smart.

I can do anything.
I have a brave heart.

5

I have rainbow power.
I zip. I zap. I zoom.

When I use my power,
things around me bloom.

Noodles is my sidekick.
He is a SUPER pug.

He is very helpful.

He also loves to hug.

If you need a hero,
we'll be there right away.

With my magic curls,
I always save the day!

A Super Birthday Cake

Lizzie planned a party.
We will have so much fun.

It's her kitty's birthday.
Waffles is turning one!

Lizzie baked a cake.
It looks just like a fish.

One candle on the top
so Waffles can make a wish.

Waffles is excited.
He jumps to see the cake.

He soars up to the top
and crashes by mistake.

The fish cake goes flying.
It sails across the room.

It lands on the sofa
upside down with a boom!

Truly to the rescue.
I need to save the day!

I'll use my rainbow power
to fix this right away.

My curly hair twinkles
while I make the magic cake.

It's a rainbow full of colors.
It takes no time to bake.

Now the cake is ready.
Waffles wants to eat.

While we sing the song,
he gobbles up the treat.

It's time to celebrate
with Waffles and my pup.

The balloons get twisted.
Oh no! He's floating up!

He flies out the window.
Sir Noodles tries to tug.

The balloons float away,
with the cat and the pug!

"Oh no!" Lizzie cries.
"What on earth will we do?"

I say, "I will save them,
but I need your help, too!"

"How can I help?" she asks.

"I am not super like you."

"I do not have a cape."

"I'm afraid to fly, too."

I say, "You can do it!
You are strong and smart."

"Just believe in yourself.
Brave comes from your heart."

Lizzie finds a cape.

My curls begin to glow.

We give our capes a twirl.
Up and away we go!

My curls sparkle and shine.
We hold hands and we fly.

We pass a puffy cloud,
then spy them in the sky!

Lizzie saves Sir Noodles.
Waffles comes with me.

I grab the last few strings.
We all cheer, "Yippee!"

We used our brave hearts.
And my magic curls.

We are strong and smart.
We are SUPER GIRLS!

About the Creators

Kelly Greenawalt is the mother of six amazing kids. She lives in Texas with her family. Her superpower is having a BIG imagination. It helps her write stories that are fun to read. Princess Truly was inspired by her oldest daughters, Calista and Kaia, who are smart and strong super girls.

Amariah Rauscher likes to read many books and play video games. She also likes to draw and paint. Her magical curls help her come up with exciting ideas for illustrations. Her super daughters, Jalen and Junie, are smart and artistic just like Princess Truly.

Read these picture books featuring Princess Truly!

YOU CAN DRAW PRINCESS TRULY!

1 Draw an ear, chin, and the side of Princess Truly's face. Then add her neck.

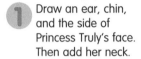

2 Add face details.

3 Draw the top and back of her hair, and a shirt. Add ringlets on her forehead.

4 Draw two butterfly hair clips, and one necklace!

5 Finish drawing her hair. Add a stripe to her shirt.

6 Color in your drawing. Don't forget the magic sparkles!

WHAT'S YOUR STORY?

Princess Truly is a super girl.
What superpowers would **you** have?
Who would your sidekick be?
How would you save the day?
Write and draw your story!

scholastic.com/acorn